初岸
true
land

与美同栖

见证树
弗罗斯特诗选

[美]罗伯特·弗罗斯特 – 著

雷格 – 译
闻燕 – 绘

国际文化出版公司
·北京·

目录
CONTENTS

02　悲哀是耐心的一种形式　　　　10　遇见弗罗斯特

The Pasture —— 002	003 —— 牧场
Into My Own —— 004	005 —— 进入我自己
A Late Walk —— 010	011 —— 一次深秋漫步
To the Thawing Wind —— 014	015 —— 致解冻的风
Mowing —— 018	019 —— 割草
October —— 020	021 —— 十月
Reluctance —— 026	027 —— 不情愿
Good Hours —— 032	033 —— 好时光
The Road Not Taken —— 036	037 —— 未走的路
Hyla Brook —— 042	043 —— 雨蛙溪
The Oven Bird —— 044	045 —— 灶鸟
Birches —— 048	049 —— 白桦树
The Cow in Apple Time —— 058	059 —— 苹果季的母牛
The Last Word of a Bluebird —— 062	063 —— 一只蓝鸫的留言

The Sound of Trees	068	069	树的声音
Fire and Ice	074	075	火与冰
Dust of Snow	076	077	雪尘
Nothing Gold Can Stay	080	081	黄金之物不久长
The Aim Was Song	082	083	目的是歌
Stopping by Woods on a Snowy Evening	088	089	雪夜林边停驻
To Earthward	092	093	向着土地
The Kitchen Chimney	100	101	厨房烟囱
Looking for a Sunset Bird in Winter	106	107	冬日黄昏寻鸟
Gathering Leaves	112	113	收集落叶
On a Tree Fallen Across the Road	118	119	关于一棵横倒在路上的树
The Need of Being Versed in Country Things	124	125	精通乡下事务之必要
A Minor Bird	130	131	一只小鸟
Tree at My Window	132	133	我窗前的树

A Winter Eden	138	139	冬日伊甸园
Acquainted with the Night	144	145	熟悉黑夜
The Last Mowing	148	149	最后的割草
The Birthplace	154	155	出生地
Sitting by a Bush in Broad Sunlight	156	157	晴日灌木林边小坐
A Leaf-Treader	162	163	踏叶人
Neither Out Far Nor In Deep	164	165	不远也不深
Beech	170	171	山毛榉
Come In	172	173	请进
A Young Birch	178	179	一棵小白桦
Away!	184	185	离去！
Forgive, O Lord...	190	191	哦主，请原谅……
In Winter in the Woods...	192	193	冬日独自在林里……

悲哀是耐心的一种形式

雷格

一

《见证树》这本诗选的举念,其实并非始于罗伯特·弗罗斯特(1874—1963)的诗。

去闻燕老师家做客,见到墙上挂着的她画的树,受到了强烈的震撼。这些树,有的昂然向天,有的被风吹弯,有的孤身映着一轮枯月,有的密密麻麻地虬结为一团——但无一例外地,它们全都没有树叶。

第一感是,这些树好像弗罗斯特笔下的树啊,寂寞、冷峻又悲哀。于是邀请闻燕老师加盟我们的"诗画系列",用她的画与弗罗斯特的诗相互映照、相互诠释、相互激发。

事情就这么成了。

二

这本诗选原本计划请杨铁军编选和翻译,可惜由于翻译版权的关系,铁军无法加盟。我写《诗歌的秘密花园:20世纪伟大诗人名作细读》时,为了解读弗罗斯特的诗,也曾翻译过《精通乡下事务之必要》等几首,感觉还不错,于是决定自己领下这个任务。

这本诗选主要收录弗罗斯特的抒情短诗,包括一些流传甚广的名作,像《未走的路》《雪夜林边停驻》《熟悉黑夜》《踏叶人》等,而且尽量多地选入了一些以树为题材的诗,最长的一首是《白桦树》。他的小戏剧诗如《雇工之死》《家葬》《小溪西流》《雪》等名作,这次则没有选入。

书名"见证树"取自弗罗斯特1942年出版的诗集《见证树》及诗集的卷首诗《山毛榉》:

> 我的假想线在树林里
> 折成方形的地方,一根铁脊
> 和一堆真正的石块已经竖起。
> 在这荒野的一角以外,
> 这些东西被运进、堆放的地方,
> 一棵树,曾经被割出深深的伤口,
> 由此标记为"见证树",
> 让我并非没有边界的证据

得以提交给记忆。
就这样真相确立并得到证明,
尽管处于黑暗和怀疑的环境之中——
尽管为一个怀疑的世界所包围。

所谓"见证树",指的是人们勘察土地时,会将一棵树剥去部分树皮、刻上标记,作为界桩,又称为"标志树"。"见证树"在这里是人与自然关系的一个隐喻,代表着人对自然的伤害,同时也暗示了人本身所受到的伤害。

翻译弗罗斯特的诗,的确堪称一段愉快的经历,但如何把握那些流畅的诗句背后复杂的心境,如何把握弗罗斯特独特的灵魂,却不是件简单的事。

三

弗罗斯特享寿甚久,阅历更是丰富,人生的几种极致悲苦,如幼年丧父、中年丧妻、老年丧子,他几乎都经受过。这构成了他精神和作品的悲哀底色,即便是他一生所取得的巨大成就——四获普利策诗歌奖、享有44个荣誉学位、成为美国最受大众爱戴的诗人——也不能抵消和抹杀。

尽管弗罗斯特以"自然诗人""乡村诗人"名世,他却不是一个纯粹的自然之子、乡村之子。他出生在美国西海岸的摩登城市旧金山,11岁时父亲病故,一家人迫于生计,千里扶柩横跨整个美国,去新英格兰投奔他乡下的祖父母。这种由城市向乡村的史诗般退却与回溯,成为他人生哲学和美学原则形成的一个重大转折点。

新英格兰地区风光很美,实际上自然条件比较恶劣,气温偏低,冬季漫长多雪,不太适于农业耕作。新英格兰以严酷的自然环境接纳了弗罗斯特,也将新英格兰人在严酷的生存环境中形成的精神气质、人际关系模式和道德规范交付给了他:坚韧、骄傲、讲原则,看透生死,视荣誉为生命。

率先代表新英格兰考验和接纳弗罗斯特的,正是那里的树、那里的树林。比如白桦树,在寒冷的冬季成为无聊的男孩子们打发寂寞时光的玩具,被他们荡得东倒西歪。弗罗斯特也是其中一员。他坦陈,《白桦树》一诗所写的白桦树就是"我在新罕布什尔塞勒姆镇上中学时在学校附近荡过的树":

> 我自己也曾是个白桦树荡手。
> 所以我也梦想着回去再荡一次。

如果说白桦树还多少意味着对美好的少年时光的追怀,树林则一直构成对弗罗斯特勇气和智慧的严峻考验。他从小害怕黑暗,为了克服这种恐惧,常常自发地在深夜走进幽深的树林,在黑暗中体味无尽的孤独。树林的黑暗与孤独是绝对的、强大的,对他形成了难以抗拒的诱惑,是否勇敢地走进去,这一点让他纠结一生。比如在《雪夜林边停驻》一诗中,尽管树林充满美、神秘和危险的丰富意涵,他也只是作为一个他者驻足旁观,最终抵御住了这种诱惑:

> 林子可爱、昏暗而深邃,
> 可我还有着约定要信守,
> 临睡前还有几英里路要走,
> 临睡前还有几英里路要走。

而在《请进》一诗中，画眉的歌声为树林的幽深与神秘增添了更多的魅力，向他发出"请进"的邀约：

> 远在廊柱撑起的黑暗中
> 画眉在鸣啭——
> 几乎像一声召唤，邀请
> 进入黑暗哀叹。

但弗罗斯特仍然抵御住诱惑，拒绝了邀约。布罗茨基曾有一篇长文《悲伤与理智》专门细读、讨论这首诗，并令人信服地指出，整首诗就是对诗题《请进》的翻译，其含义或许就是"死亡"。这样一来，弗罗斯特作为个体与树林的对峙就升格为人与自然的结构性矛盾，冲突双方旗鼓相当，他们之间的角力天然而持久，并不涉及道德评判和伦理困境。

于是，在这样一种自然观念引领下，他可以干脆地拒绝落叶的死亡邀约：

> 它们对我内心的逃犯讲话，就好像树叶对树叶。
> 它们敲打我眼睑、碰触我嘴唇，发出悲伤的邀约。
> 但没有这样的道理，因为它们要走，我就得坠落。
> ——《踏叶人》

也可以残酷地向枫树抡起利斧而毫无心理负担：

> 冬日独自在林里
> 我准备对树不利。

> 我标好一棵枫树给自己
> 然后将它砍倒在地。
> ——《冬日独自在林里……》

他认为，树遭到砍伐并不是"自然的失利"，他离开树林也不是"失利"，并且自然而然地期待着对自然的"再一次打击"。

四

弗罗斯特的人生哲学与他的自然观念一脉相承。用他自己的话说就是："无论多么悲痛也不抱怨，悲而不怨。"

他在致友人的信中坦言："我并不想看见世界、美国甚至纽约被变得更好……我不想让这个世界变成对诗歌来说更安全或更舒适的地方。"也就是说，他无意改变这个世界，因为改变世界的想法是出于不满，而他不喜欢不满，他喜欢的是悲哀——"不满是急躁的一种形式。悲哀是耐心的一种形式。"他甚至半开玩笑半认真地说，希望"把不满限制在小说散文中，而允许诗歌流着泪去走它自己的路"。

关于自己对于悲哀的信念，弗罗斯特还说："没有任何东西会使我放弃我拥有的坚忍不拔的悲哀。"他的诗《精通乡下事务之必要》就为这种"坚忍不拔的悲哀"做了非常精彩的旁注：

> 它们真的没什么可悲伤的。
> 尽管幸存的鸟巢让它们欢喜，
> 人还是得精通些乡下事务

才不至于相信菲比鹟会哭泣。

人如果精通些乡下事务,就不至于一厢情愿地一再误读自然,以为鸟儿和人一样多愁善感、一样虚妄。"坚忍不拔的悲哀"是弗罗斯特在新英格兰的生存搏斗中习得的人生态度,那是对悲哀的安之若素,那是务实、达观和无畏。

艾略特应该就是看到了弗罗斯特的这种特质,才会做出以下判断:"有一种地方感情可以被普遍接受,那就是但丁对佛罗伦萨的感情、莎士比亚对沃里克郡的感情、歌德对莱茵兰的感情、弗罗斯特对新英格兰的感情。他具有那种普遍性。"让弗罗斯特与三大巅峰诗人并驾齐驱,这是无上的赞誉,也是不凡的识见。

五

为《诗歌的秘密花园》写弗罗斯特时,我内心对他还有一些保留意见,特别是在他与史蒂文斯的美学拮抗中,暗暗站队史蒂文斯。现在,翻译过他的四十多首诗,我的立场悄悄发生了偏转。

针对20世纪初叶庞德、艾略特等人所倡导的诗歌变革与创新,比如不用标点、取消格律、不写格言警句、只依赖视觉意象、以"纯诗"否定内容等做法,弗罗斯特曾经打过一个著名的比方加以讽刺:不押韵的自由诗,就像是打网球时场上却没有网子。这会给人一种印象,即弗罗斯特以一种墨守成规的顽固拒斥了诗歌的现代性。但这绝对是误解。

虽然弗罗斯特的格律诗在形式上继承19世纪英国浪漫主义诗歌遗产,娴熟地使用抑扬格、五音步、双行体、尾韵,但他所独创的诗歌美学却毫不因袭，可以说真正地超迈前人。在思想层面，他的自然观念给了诗歌内容前所未有的深度；在声音层面，他冷静中浸透悲哀的节奏和语调大大降低了诗歌的调门，不再那样高蹈和夸饰，而归于可贵的诚实；在技巧层面，他充满先见之明地强调了"暗示"和"口语化"对于诗歌的极端重要性——"我坚信口语化是任何一首好诗的根，正如我坚信民族性是所有思想和艺术的根一样。"

在我看来，弗罗斯特不是一个现代主义诗人，但他是一个不折不扣的现代诗人。

对弗罗斯特的再认识让我意识到，我们对他的阅读也许还远远不够。最近开了一门线上诗歌课，要为学员选一个范本来模仿。我最终选择了弗罗斯特的《好时光》：

> 我漫步在冬日的夜晚——
> 没有同行的人可以交谈，
> 但我有排成一列的农舍，
> 它们的眼睛在雪野中闪烁。

里面有诗歌所需的全部要素，而且像一个正常人写的诗——由此想到了弗罗斯特说过的一句话："谁有权随心所欲地把玩我的诗——就是那些能按自己的方式去理解它们的正常人。"

遇见弗罗斯特

闻燕

记忆中一幅永远抹不去的画面：一个眼睛大大的孩子，手拿着一根细小的木棍儿，漫无目的地浪迹在广袤的黄土高原上。很长时间了，他固执地拒绝和人说话，甚至父母，甚至兄弟。他被一些没有答案的问题纠缠得苦恼极了：我是谁？这是哪里？我将往何处去？一份不该这个年龄所有的沉重坠着孩子的心。

那孩子又是谁呢？

2020年是让人震惊的一年。人们与一种未知的病毒猝然遭遇，高速的生活节奏终于慢下来，仿佛一台疯狂运转的机器，慢慢停止了转动，陷入寂静。徘徊在第一次空出的偌大的校园，感觉有些陌生。山坡上，树木伸展着掉光了叶子的黝黑的枯枝，向着蓝色的天空，默默无语。我喜欢这冬日卸下了一切装饰的树木，给你一个干枯的真相。天空也是。太阳也是。你以为的火，你以为的温暖，都离你远去了。这干枯，这冷，才是世间的真相。走在校园里，却仿佛穿越回童年的高原，与那个陷入无端苦恼的、无援的孩子撞了个满怀。耸峙的塬上不见同类，连发声的动物也没有。没想到，庚子的校园也有这样的时候。

忽然间却想起了罗伯特·弗罗斯特的诗……

我一度对诗有偏见，总是敬而远之。弗罗斯特的诗却让我感到亲切。每次读，都被一种无法言语的魔力抓住，一次比一次强烈。弗罗斯特的诗用自然的景观制造了一个又一个幻象。他笔下的自然表面上是美的、亲切的，却有可怕的、人类无法探测的深度。凋零的树叶、光秃秃的树、鸟儿们悲哀的叫声、镰刀的低语声……这一切的后面隐藏着一个深渊。这深渊是从哪里涌出来的呢？真相是，它就来自诗人的内心。在诗人的笔下，山冈、田野、森林，大自然的一切美好似乎只为了衬托着诗人内心的荒凉。《进入我自己》把那个深渊带到了表面。这首诗让我们看到了诗人，也是人类自我中阴暗的一面："那些黝黑的树，……不再如以往，……而是伸展开来，直至毁灭的边缘。"但诗人却渴望进入这个深渊："我不该遭到扣留，总有一天 / 我会偷偷溜走，进入它们的浩瀚……"他因为这种进入而更加笃信自己："他们不会发现，我已不再是熟识的那个他 / 只是更加笃信我全部正确的想法。"曾几何时，我也像弗罗斯特诗中的主人公一样，孤独地行走在荒野，试图进入某个不可测的东西里面。走进去，不断地走进去……借此解除内心的焦虑，在滩涂中给自己挖掘出一个可以呼吸的孔隙。在弗罗斯特的诗里，我似乎遇见了自己。有生以来，第一次对诗人深深顶礼。

我一直对冬天光秃秃的树感到着迷。枝繁叶茂的大树并不令我欣然，只有到了深秋，当它们褪去最后一片树叶，我才感到它们魅力四射。因为只有这个时候，我们才能看到树的元神。裸露的树干和枝条不再受缚于花叶的装束，肆意地在天空下伸展自己的身体，仿佛裸体的、不死的神，与冬阳嬉戏，与寒风搏战，或者默默承受着雪的重载。这种赤裸的美才是无与伦比的，超越葳蕤的春花，也超越燃烧的秋树。在萧瑟的寒风中见到这样的树，我每每莫名感动，很想静静地站在它们的旁边，让自己也变成一棵树……弗罗斯特笔下的自然向我显现的就是这种冬树的赤裸的、揭示了真相的魅力。我忽然想，我能不能用一些冬树的画幅来诠释这个亲切而又神秘的诗人呢？弗罗斯特在多首诗中描绘过树的形象，被暴风雪折断的树、与最后一片落叶纠缠的树、孤独地站在墙角的树、窗前的树、休眠的树、长满了大山膝头的树、见证树……就像《进入我自己》中的树一样，这些树都是诗人自我的写像。那首《冬日独自在林里……》让我吃惊，当一个树木的对话者竟然说出："冬日独自在林里／我准备对树不利。／我标好一棵枫树给自己／然后将它砍倒在地……"这倒地的也是诗人自己，他是在自己的身上砍伐。这首诗让我看到了诗人的绝望和疯狂。我本来喜好画树，喜欢倾听树的呢喃，好奇林中的黑暗。弗罗斯特这些写树的诗，再次唤起我画树的热情。但面对弗罗斯特的诗，手中的笔却显得无力。我画了一张又一张，撕了一张又一张，留下来的也没好到哪儿去。诗的意境离我的画幅依然遥远，依然不可捉摸。甚至比我画下它们之前更加遥远。

一个朋友看到我的树，发出疑问："你是有多么绝望，才会画出这样的树？"虽然我不是一个乐观的人，听到这样的话，也不免悚然。我的画真那么绝望吗？面对倒地的树，弗罗斯特说："我不会将一棵树的倒地／看作自然的失利，／我的退却也并非失利，／而是为了再一次打击。"这是诗人面对失败的态度。《离去！》写到死亡："不要以为我离家／是为了外面的黑暗",“我也许还会回转，／假如我不满意／从自己的死亡里面／学到的东西"。以一种从容的幽默面对失败乃至死亡，有人说是诗人的智慧，在我看来不如说是诗人的一种自我保护。弗罗斯特是一个善于隐瞒的人吧。他的疯狂，他的绝望，都被一种亲切的语调和朴实的假象隐藏起来。这是为了自我保护，也是为了保护别人。读着弗罗斯特的诗，我们的心也受到了抚慰。

若要成长，需要封存绝望。谁这么说过呢？想不起来了。也许是我们的心吧。让我们绝望的是理智，让我们活下去的是心。心是能量。它不断地泵出血，泵出热情。它用能量向理智隐瞒了生存的真相。所以我们还能活下去。弗罗斯特还能写诗。我还能画下这些树。年轻人还能恋爱。

感谢上帝，让我们拥有一颗心。

感谢上帝，我还拥有一颗心。

The Pasture

I'm going out to clean the pasture spring;

I'll only stop to rake the leaves away

(And wait to watch the water clear, I may):

I shan't be gone long.—You come too.

I'm going out to fetch the little calf

That's standing by the mother. It's so young

It totters when she licks it with her tongue.

I shan't be gone long.—You come too.

牧场

我要出去清理那牧场的水泉;

我只是停下来,耙掉落叶

(也许还会等着看泉水清澈):

我不会去很久。—— 你也来吧。

我要出去带回那小牛犊,

它站在妈妈身旁,这样幼弱,

妈妈伸舌头舔得它直趔趄。

我不会去很久。—— 你也来吧。

Into My Own

One of my wishes is that those dark trees,

So old and firm they scarcely show the breeze,

Were not, as 'twere, the merest mask of gloom,

But stretched away unto the edge of doom.

I should not be withheld but that some day

Into their vastness I should steal away,

Fearless of ever finding open land,

Or highway where the slow wheel pours the sand.

I do not see why I should e'er turn back,

Or those should not set forth upon my track

To overtake me, who should miss me here

And long to know if still I held them dear.

进入我自己

我的一个愿望是,那些黝黑的树,

古老坚实得几乎透不进风的树,

不再如以往,只是幽暗的假面,

而是伸展开来,直至毁灭的边缘。

我不该遭到扣留,总有一天

我会偷偷溜走,进入它们的浩瀚,

不畏惧总是发现开阔地,

或是公路,有缓慢的车轮泼洒沙子。

我想不出为什么我该回头,

为什么那些人不沿着我的足迹走

并且赶超我,他们在这里将我错失,

还渴望知道,我是否仍对他们珍视。

They would not find me changed from him they knew —

Only more sure of all I thought was true.

他们不会发现，我已不再是熟识的那个他——
只是更加笃信我全部正确的想法。

A Late Walk

When I go up through the mowing field,

    The headless aftermath,

Smooth-laid like thatch with the heavy dew,

    Half closes the garden path.

And when I come to the garden ground,

    The whir of sober birds

Up from the tangle of withered weeds

    Is sadder than any words.

A tree beside the wall stands bare,

    But a leaf that lingered brown,

Disturbed, I doubt not, by my thought,

    Comes softly rattling down.

一次深秋漫步

当我穿行在割过草的牧场,
　　那砍了头的再生草
平顺如茅草屋顶带着重露,
　　半掩着花园小道。

当我踏上花园地面,
　　缠结的枯草丛传来
清醒的鸟儿们的嗡鸣,
　　比任何言语都悲哀。

墙边光秃秃地立着一棵树,
　　只挂着一片褐色枯叶,
我毫不怀疑,它被我的思绪惊扰,
　　唰的一下轻轻飘落。

I end not far from my going forth,

By picking the faded blue

Of the last remaining aster flower

To carry again to you.

我走不多远就停住脚步,

　　摘下最后一枝

紫菀花褪了色的蓝,

　　再一次带回给你。

To the Thawing Wind

Come with rain, O loud Southwester!

Bring the singer, bring the nester;

Give the buried flower a dream;

Make the settled snowbank steam;

Find the brown beneath the white;

But whate'er you do tonight,

Bathe my window, make it flow,

Melt it as the ice will go;

Melt the glass and leave the sticks

Like a hermit's crucifix;

Burst into my narrow stall;

Swing the picture on the wall;

Run the rattling pages o'er;

Scatter poems on the floor;

Turn the poet out of door.

Robert Frost
A Witness Tree

致解冻的风

带着雨水来,哦,喧嚣的西南风!

带来那歌唱者,带来那筑巢工;

给那深埋的花朵以梦寐,

让那安稳的雪堆化成溪水;

发现那白色下面的褐色;

但无论你今夜做什么,

请冲刷我的窗户,让它流动,

融化它,就像融化冰;

融化玻璃,把窗棂留下,

好像一位隐士的十字架;

吹进我狭仄的棚屋;

摇晃墙上挂着的画幅;

把书页翻动得哗啦响;

让诗笺散落一地;

把那诗人赶出门去。

Mowing

There was never a sound beside the wood but one,

And that was my long scythe whispering to the ground.

What was it it whispered? I knew not well myself;

Perhaps it was something about the heat of the sun,

Something, perhaps, about the lack of sound—

And that was why it whispered and did not speak.

It was no dream of the gift of idle hours,

Or easy gold at the hand of fay or elf:

Anything more than the truth would have seemed too weak

To the earnest love that laid the swale in rows,

Not without feeble-pointed spikes of flowers

(Pale orchises), and scared a bright green snake.

The fact is the sweetest dream that labor knows.

My long scythe whispered and left the hay to make.

Robert Frost
A Witness Tree

割草

树林边向来安静,只有一种声音,

那是我的长镰刀对着大地低语。

它低语些什么?我自己也不很清楚;

也许说的是太阳的炎热,

也许说的是这儿阒寂无声——

那就是它为什么低语,不高声讲话。

那不是梦想着不劳而获,

或是从仙女精灵手中白得金子:

任何超出真实的东西,在洼地里排成列的

真诚的爱面前都显得太无力,

虽然不免伤到娇弱的花穗

(苍白的兰花),吓到一条晶亮的青蛇。

事实乃是劳动所知晓的最甜蜜的梦。

我的长镰刀低语,留下干草晒成。

October

O hushed October morning mild,

Thy leaves have ripened to the fall;

Tomorrow's wind, if it be wild,

Should waste them all.

The crows above the forest call;

Tomorrow they may form and go.

O hushed October morning mild,

Begin the hours of this day slow.

Make the day seem to us less brief.

Hearts not averse to being beguiled,

Beguile us in the way you know.

Release one leaf at break of day;

At noon release another leaf;

One from our trees, one far away.

Retard the sun with gentle mist;

十月

哦,十月的清晨寂静而煦和,

你的树叶已成熟到可以飘落;

明天的风若是来得狂烈,

会把它们全都吹掉。

乌鸦在森林上空鸣叫;

明天它们也许会集结,离去。

哦,十月的清晨寂静而煦和,

慢慢将一天的时辰开启。

让这一天对我们似乎没那么短暂。

心并不反感被欺骗,

骗我们,请用你熟知的方式。

破晓时分掉落一片树叶;

到正午再掉落一片;

一片飘下我们的树,一片落得老远。

用轻柔的雾将太阳拖住;

Enchant the land with amethyst.

Slow, slow!

For the grapes' sake, if they were all,

Whose leaves already are burnt with frost,

Whose clustered fruit must else be lost —

For the grapes' sake along the wall.

用紫水晶向这土地施加魔术。

慢点,慢点!

为了葡萄,哪怕只为了葡萄,

它们的叶子已经被寒霜灼伤,

不如此,它们的串串果实也肯定丢光——

为了沿墙攀缘的葡萄。

Reluctance

Out through the fields and the woods
    And over the walls I have wended;
I have climbed the hills of view
    And looked at the world, and descended;
I have come by the highway home,
    And lo, it is ended.

The leaves are all dead on the ground,
    Save those that the oak is keeping
To ravel them one by one
    And let them go scraping and creeping
Out over the crusted snow,
    When others are sleeping.

Robert Frost
A Witness Tree

不情愿

我曾穿过田野和树林,
　　　也曾翻过墙垣;
我曾登上视野开阔的山冈
　　　看这世界,然后下山;
我曾沿着公路回家,
　　　瞧,这就是终点。

树叶都已枯死在地面,
　　　除了橡树还保留的那些,
它要一片一片卸下它们,
　　　让它们在结了冰壳的
雪上刮擦、匍匐,
　　　当其他树叶正在安歇。

And the dead leaves lie huddled and still,

    No longer blown hither and thither;

The last lone aster is gone;

    The flowers of the witch hazel wither;

The heart is still aching to seek,

    But the feet question "Whither?"

Ah, when to the heart of man

    Was it ever less than a treason

To go with the drift of things,

    To yield with a grace to reason,

And bow and accept the end

    Of a love or a season?

枯叶簇拥在一起静止，

　　不再被吹来吹去；

最后一朵寂寞的紫菀花已消逝；

　　金缕梅的花儿枯死；

心还在苦苦寻找，

　　双脚却问："去哪里？"

啊，对人类的心来说

　　什么时候这才不算是背弃，

如果顺势而行，

　　优雅地屈从于理智，

还有，躬身接受一场恋爱

　　或一个季节的终止？

Good Hours

I had for my winter evening walk—

No one at all with whom to talk,

But I had the cottages in a row

Up to their shining eyes in snow.

And I thought I had the folk within:

I had the sound of a violin;

I had a glimpse through curtain laces

Of youthful forms and youthful faces.

I had such company outward bound.

I went till there were no cottages found.

I turned and repented, but coming back

I saw no window but that was black.

好时光

我漫步在冬日的夜晚——

没有同行的人可以交谈,

但我有排成一列的农舍,

它们的眼睛在雪野中闪烁。

我想我还有屋子里的乡亲:

我有一把小提琴的乐音;

我透过窗帘的花边瞥见

年轻的身形和年轻的脸。

我外出竟有如此的陪伴。

我一直走到不再有农舍出现。

我转过身又懊悔,但我返回

却看不见窗户,只有一片漆黑。

Over the snow my creaking feet

Disturbed the slumbering village street

Like profanation, by your leave,

At ten o'clock of a winter eve.

走过雪地我的脚步嘎吱作响,

搅扰了沉睡中的乡村街巷,

好像亵渎一般,真是抱歉,

在这十点钟的冬日夜晚。

The Road Not Taken

Two roads diverged in a yellow wood,

And sorry I could not travel both

And be one traveler, long I stood

And looked down one as far as I could

To where it bent in the undergrowth;

Then took the other, as just as fair,

And having perhaps the better claim,

Because it was grassy and wanted wear;

Though as for that, the passing there

Had worn them really about the same,

And both that morning equally lay

In leaves no step had trodden black.

Oh, I kept the first for another day!

Robert Frost
A Witness Tree

未走的路

金黄的树林中岔开两条路,
很遗憾我是孤身旅行
不能两条都走,我久久驻足
沿着其中的一条极目望向深处
直到它拐进了灌木丛;

然后走上另一条,它同样适合,
也许选择它是更好的主张,
因为它杂草丛生,需要踩磨;
不过说到这一点,过路者
踩磨它们的程度差不多一样,

而那天早上两条路同样安卧于
落叶之下,还没有脚步来踩黑。
哦,我把第一条路留待他日!

Yet knowing how way leads on to way,

I doubted if I should ever come back.

I shall be telling this with a sigh

Somewhere ages and ages hence:

Two roads diverged in a wood, and I—

I took the one less traveled by,

And that has made all the difference.

不过明白了路和路如何相联系,

我怀疑自己是否还会返回。

很久很久以后在某处

我将旧事重提,一声叹息:

两条路在树林中岔开,而我——

我选择了少有人走的那条路,

这造成了此后所有的差异。

Hyla Brook

By June our brook's run out of song and speed.

Sought for much after that, it will be found

Either to have gone groping underground

(And taken with it all the Hyla breed

That shouted in the mist a month ago,

Like ghost of sleigh bells in a ghost of snow) —

Or flourished and come up in jewelweed,

Weak foliage that is blown upon and bent,

Even against the way its waters went.

Its bed is left a faded paper sheet

Of dead leaves stuck together by the heat —

A brook to none but who remember long.

This as it will be seen is other far

Than with brooks taken otherwise in song.

We love the things we love for what they are.

雨蛙溪

到六月我们的小溪就不再歌唱和奔流。

过一阵子再去找，就会发现

它或者潜入地下，摸索向前

（把所有种类的雨蛙都带走，

一个月前它们还在迷雾中喧鸣，

好像雪的幽灵里雪橇铃铛的幽灵①）——

或者开了花，随凤仙草冒出头，

柔弱的茎叶被风吹弯，甚至

逆着溪水曾经流淌的方向弯曲。

它废弃的溪床成了一张褪色的纸，

那是败叶热得粘连在一起——

唯有记得久的人，才知这是一条小溪。

如我们所见，它远胜于

那些歌唱着流向别处的小溪。

我们热爱事物，终究爱其所是。

---

① 雨蛙的鸣叫声近似铃声。

The Oven Bird

There is a singer everyone has heard,

Loud, a mid-summer and a mid-wood bird,

Who makes the solid tree trunks sound again.

He says that leaves are old and that for flowers

Mid-summer is to spring as one to ten.

He says the early petal-fall is past,

When pear and cherry bloom went down in showers

On sunny days a moment overcast;

And comes that other fall we name the fall.

He says the highway dust is over all.

The bird would cease and be as other birds

But that he knows in singing not to sing.

The question that he frames in all but words

Is what to make of a diminished thing.

灶鸟①

有一位歌手人人都曾听到，

嗓门亮，是一只仲夏的林中鸟，

能让坚实的树干再次发出声音。

他说树叶老了，而对于花儿来说，

仲夏之于春天，如一分之于十分。

他说早期的落花季已过，

当艳阳天里有一刻密布阴云，

梨花和樱桃花如阵雨纷纷凋落；

然后是另一次凋落，我们称之为秋天②。

他说公路上到处是滚滚尘烟。

这只鸟会息声，像其他鸟一样，

但是他懂得不唱的歌唱。

他唯独不用言语提出的那个问题

就是如何理解一件事物的式微。

---

① 灶鸟在地面上用枯草筑巢，形似炉灶，故名。
② "凋落"和"秋天"在美国英语中是同一个词：fall。

Birches

When I see birches bend to left and right

Across the lines of straighter darker trees,

I like to think some boy's been swinging them.

But swinging doesn't bend them down to stay

As ice storms do. Often you must have seen them

Loaded with ice a sunny winter morning

After a rain. They click upon themselves

As the breeze rises, and turn many-colored

As the stir cracks and crazes their enamel.

Soon the sun's warmth makes them shed crystal shells

Shattering and avalanching on the snow crust—

Such heaps of broken glass to sweep away

You'd think the inner dome of heaven had fallen.

They are dragged to the withered bracken by the load,

And they seem not to break; though once they are bowed

Robert Frost
A Witness Tree

白桦树

当我看见白桦树弯向左和右,

横过更直更黑的树的行列,

我认为某个男孩曾经悠荡过它们。

但悠荡不至于让它们弯下去停住,

一如冰暴① 所为。你肯定常常见到它们

在雨后一个阳光明媚的冬日早晨

结满了冰凌。轻风吹来

它们身上就喀拉作响,当这震动

让那釉质开裂,就变得五彩缤纷。

不久阳光的温热让它们的水晶壳剥落,

摔碎在雪壳上,好像雪崩 ——

有这么一大堆碎玻璃要打扫,

你会以为是天国的内穹顶塌了。

重压之下,它们被拖向枯萎的蕨草,

看上去并不会折断;不过一旦长时间

---

① 冰暴是寒冷季节的一种暴风雨,降下的雨接触任何物体都会立刻冻结。

So low for long, they never right themselves:

You may see their trunks arching in the woods

Years afterwards, trailing their leaves on the ground

Like girls on hands and knees that throw their hair

Before them over their heads to dry in the sun.

But I was going to say when Truth broke in

With all her matter of fact about the ice storm,

I should prefer to have some boy bend them

As he went out and in to fetch the cows —

Some boy too far from town to learn baseball,

Whose only play was what he found himself,

Summer or winter, and could play alone.

One by one he subdued his father's trees

By riding them down over and over again

Until he took the stiffness out of them,

弯得如此之低，就再也不能自己挺直：

你可以看见树干在随后的年月里

在树林中弯成拱形，树叶拖在地面上，

就像姑娘们手脚伏地，秀发

从头顶甩到前面，在阳光中晒干。

但我要说，当真理闯入，

说明关于冰暴的全部事实，

我仍然相信是某个男孩压弯了它们，

当他进进出出牵牛的时候——

某个离城市太远学不到棒球的男孩，

他唯一的游戏是自己发明的，

无论冬夏，都可以一个人玩。

一棵接一棵，他制伏了他父亲的树，

一遍遍地骑着它们下坠，

直到他抽去了它们的硬度，

And not one but hung limp, not one was left

For him to conquer. He learned all there was

To learn about not launching out too soon

And so not carrying the tree away

Clear to the ground. He always kept his poise

To the top branches, climbing carefully

With the same pains you use to fill a cup

Up to the brim, and even above the brim.

Then he flung outward, feet first, with a swish,

Kicking his way down through the air to the ground.

So was I once myself a swinger of birches.

And so I dream of going back to be.

It's when I'm weary of considerations,

And life is too much like a pathless wood

Where your face burns and tickles with the cobwebs

没有一棵不是软趴趴地垂下，没有一棵

幸免于他的征服。 他学到了所有

可能的办法，不要开始得太快，

以免完全将树扳到

地面上。 他总是保持平衡

爬上顶部的枝杈，爬得小心翼翼，

带着那种你斟满杯子到杯沿

甚至高过杯沿的小心劲儿。

然后他向外一荡，双脚在前，嗖的一下，

一路踢蹬着从空中落到地面。

我自己也曾是个白桦树荡手。

所以我也梦想着回去再荡一次。

那是我对深思熟虑厌倦了的时候，

生活太像一片没有路的树林，

在里面，你的脸撞上蜘蛛网

Broken across it, and one eye is weeping

From a twig's having lashed across it open.

I'd like to get away from earth awhile

And then come back to it and begin over.

May no fate willfully misunderstand me

And half grant what I wish and snatch me away

Not to return. Earth's the right place for love:

I don't know where it's likely to go better.

I'd like to go by climbing a birch tree,

And climb black branches up a snow-white trunk

Toward heaven, till the tree could bear no more,

But dipped its top and set me down again.

That would be good both going and coming back.

One could do worse than be a swinger of birches.

而发烧发痒，一只眼睛

因为睁开时被小树枝抽到而流泪。

我真想离开大地片刻，

然后回来，重新开始。

但愿命运不会存心误解我，

只成全我一半心愿，把我抓走

不放回来。大地是爱的最佳地点：

我不知道还有什么更好的去处。

我愿意爬着一棵白桦树前往，

攀着黑色枝杈，沿着雪白的树干

直上天空，直到树再也承受不住，

只好垂下树梢，再次把我放下。

那样的离去和返回都很好。

一个人所为，可能比白桦树荡手更糟。

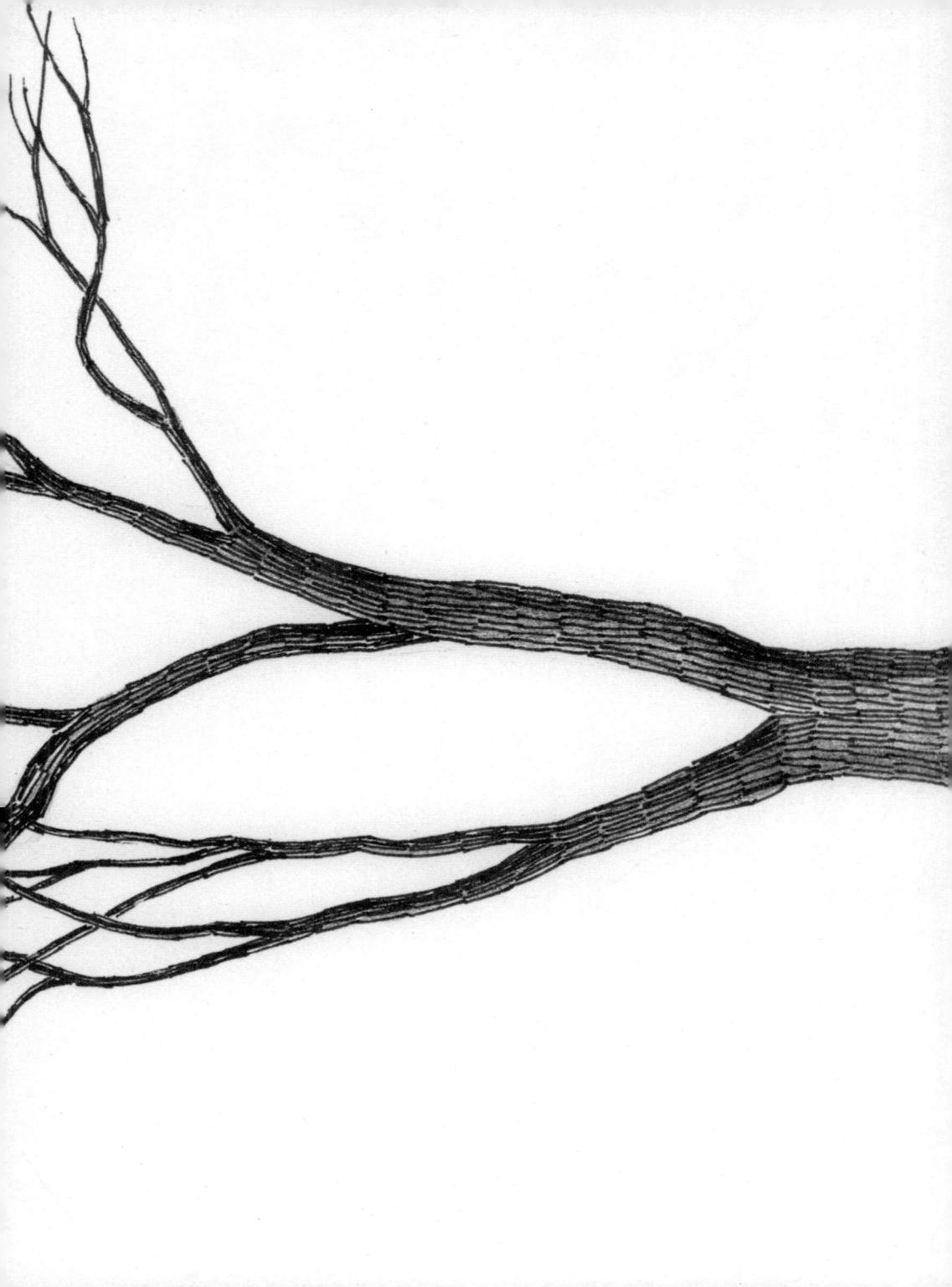

The Cow in Apple Time

Something inspires the only cow of late

To make no more of a wall than an open gate,

And think no more of wall-builders than fools.

Her face is flecked with pomace and she drools

A cider syrup. Having tasted fruit,

She scorns a pasture withering to the root.

She runs from tree to tree where lie and sweeten

The windfalls spiked with stubble and worm-eaten.

She leaves them bitten when she has to fly.

She bellows on a knoll against the sky.

Her udder shrivels and the milk goes dry.

苹果季的母牛

近来有什么事刺激了唯一的母牛,

她觉得墙无非是大门敞着口,

砌墙人也不过是些傻瓜。

她脸上沾着苹果渣,流下

苹果汁。一旦有鲜果可尝,

她便看不上那枯萎至根的草场。

她在树和树之间穿梭,树下躺着

残枝戳过、虫子蛀过的甘甜落果。

她逃走时把咬过的果子一丢。

她在土丘上向天长吼。

她的乳房干瘪,乳汁枯竭。

ns a pasture

g to the root.

 from tree

here lie and

lfalls spiked

ble and

ten.

s them

en she has

ws on a

inst the sky.

er shrivels

ilk goes

The Last Word of a Bluebird
As told to a child

As I went out a Crow

In a low voice said, "Oh,

I was looking for you.

How do you do?

I just came to tell you

To tell Lesley (will you?)

That her little Bluebird

Wanted me to bring word

That the north wind last night

That made the stars bright

And made ice on the trough

Almost made him cough

His tail feathers off.

He just had to fly!

But he sent her Good-by,

一只蓝鸲的留言
给一个孩子的话

我出门时一只乌鸦

低声说:"哦,

我正找你呢。

你好吗?

我来是请你

转告莱斯莉①(你会吧?)

她的小小蓝鸲鸟

让我把口信带到,

北风昨天晚上

吹得星星更亮,

让冰结满水槽,

也让他差点咳掉

尾巴上的羽毛。

他只好飞走了!

但他向她道别,

---

① 莱斯莉,弗罗斯特的大女儿。

And said to be good,

And wear her red hood,

And look for the skunk tracks

In the snow with an ax —

And do everything!

And perhaps in the spring

He would come back and sing."

请她把自己照顾好,

戴上她的红帽,

拿着一把斧子在雪地里

寻找臭鼬的踪迹——

事事如意!

也许来年春上

他会回来歌唱。"

The Sound of Trees

I wonder about the trees.

Why do we wish to bear

Forever the noise of these

More than another noise

So close to our dwelling place?

We suffer them by the day

Till we lose all measure of pace,

And fixity in our joys,

And acquire a listening air.

They are that that talks of going

But never gets away;

And that talks no less for knowing,

As it grows wiser and older,

That now it means to stay.

My feet tug at the floor

树的声音

这些树让我纳闷。

我们为什么希望

永远忍受这些树的声音,

对离我们的居所如此之近的

另一种声音却受不了?

我们吃尽苦头,直到那一天

我们失去了所有的步调

和我们恒定不变的快乐,

养成了一副倾听的模样。

它们是那种总说要走

却永远不动身的货色;

成长得更智慧更老以后,

它们居然还说要去了解,

而现在这意味着留下。

有时我从窗口或门口

And my head sways to my shoulder

Sometimes when I watch trees sway,

From the window or the door.

I shall set forth for somewhere,

I shall make the reckless choice

Some day when they are in voice

And tossing so as to scare

The white clouds over them on.

I shall have less to say,

But I shall be gone.

看着这些树摇曳,

就把双脚在地板上拖,

把脑袋垂向肩头。

如果有一天它们发出声音,

摇曳着去惊吓

它们头顶的白色云朵,

我就起身去往某个地方,

我要作出不计后果的选择。

我没什么话可说,

但我要走了。

Fire and Ice

Some say the world will end in fire,

Some say in ice.

From what I've tasted of desire

I hold with those who favor fire.

But if it had to perish twice,

I think I know enough of hate

To say that for destruction ice

Is also great

And would suffice.

火与冰

有人说世界将终结于火,

有人说终结于冰。

从我品尝欲望的感受来说

我支持那些火的钟情者。

但如果两次灭亡已经注定,

我想凭我对仇恨的认识

可以说,行毁灭之事的冰

有着同样的伟力

而且够用。

Dust of Snow

The way a crow

Shook down on me

The dust of snow

From a hemlock tree

Has given my heart

A change of mood

And saved some part

Of a day I had rued.

Robert Frost
A Witness Tree

雪尘

一只乌鸦如何

从一棵铁杉树上

将雪尘抖落

到我的身上

已经让我

心情为之一变

多少挽回了

我懊悔的一天。

Nothing Gold Can Stay

Nature's first green is gold,

Her hardest hue to hold.

Her early leaf's a flower;

But only so an hour.

Then leaf subsides to leaf.

So Eden sank to grief,

So dawn goes down to day.

Nothing gold can stay.

黄金之物不久长

自然的第一抹绿是黄金①,

她这般色彩最难留存。

她初生的叶子是花;

但只有一小时的风华。

随后叶子消退为叶子。

于是伊甸园陷入悲戚,

于是黎明向白日沉降。

一切黄金之物都不久长。

---

① 似指叶子初生时那种嫩黄的状态。

The Aim Was Song

Before man came to blow it right

    The wind once blew itself untaught,

And did its loudest day and night

    In any rough place where it caught.

Man came to tell it what was wrong:

    It hadn't found the place to blow;

It blew too hard — the aim was song.

    And listen — how it ought to go!

He took a little in his mouth,

    And held it long enough for north

To be converted into south,

    And then by measure blew it forth.

目的是歌

在人来正确吹它之前

  风曾无师自通地吹起,

然后日日夜夜竭力嘶喊

  在它遇到的一切粗砺之地。

人来告诉它如何出了错:

  它没有找对该吹的地方;

它吹得太重了 —— 目的是歌。

  听听 —— 到底应该怎样!

他吸了一小股风在口中,

  因为憋得足够持久

朔风变成了熏风,

  然后按照韵律吹出。

By measure. It was word and note,

    The wind the wind had meant to be—

A little through the lips and throat.

    The aim was song—the wind could see.

按照韵律。那就是歌词和乐音，

风啊风本来就应该 ——

一点点穿过喉咙和嘴唇。

目的是歌 —— 风会明白。

an

blow

ce

lf

t,

its

day

t

ough

ere it

Stopping by Woods on a Snowy Evening

Whose woods these are I think I know.

His house is in the village, though;

He will not see me stopping here

To watch his woods fill up with snow.

My little horse must think it queer

To stop without a farmhouse near

Between the woods and frozen lake

The darkest evening of the year.

He gives his harness bells a shake

To ask if there is some mistake.

The only other sound's the sweep

Of easy wind and downy flake.

Robert Frost
A Witness Tree

雪夜林边停驻

林子是谁的我想我知悉。
不过他的宅子是在村里;
他不会看到我在此停歇
望着他积满白雪的林子。

我的小马一定感到不解,
停脚处附近并没有农舍,
在林子和冰封的湖当中,
在这一年里最黑的一夜。

他抖了抖挽具上的响铃,
问我是否出了什么毛病。
除此之外的声音就只有
轻风吹拂和雪花飘落声。

The woods are lovely, dark, and deep,

But I have promises to keep,

And miles to go before I sleep,

And miles to go before I sleep.

林子可爱、昏暗而深幽,

可我还有着约定要信守,

临睡前还有几英里路要走,

临睡前还有几英里路要走。

To Earthward

Love at the lips was touch

As sweet as I could bear;

And once that seemed too much;

I lived on air

That crossed me from sweet things,

The flow of—was it musk

From hidden grapevine springs

Downhill at dusk?

I had the swirl and ache

From sprays of honeysuckle

That when they're gathered shake

Dew on the knuckle.

向着土地

嘴唇上的爱曾是我

能够承受的香甜碰触；

它似乎一度甜得太过；

我的生活依赖于

从香甜之物扑向我的气息，

不绝如缕 —— 莫非

是山下隐秘的葡萄丛里

薄暮时分的麝香味？

我曾被忍冬的花枝

弄得眩晕和痛苦，

那是我采集它们时

抖落在指节上的花露。

I craved strong sweets, but those

Seemed strong when I was young;

The petal of the rose

It was that stung.

Now no joy but lacks salt,

That is not dashed with pain

And weariness and fault;

I crave the stain

Of tears, the aftermark

Of almost too much love,

The sweet of bitter bark

And burning clove.

我曾渴望浓烈的香甜，但那香甜

似乎在我年少时才浓烈；

玫瑰的花瓣

那样刺痛我。

如今的欢乐没有不缺盐少味的，

全都用痛苦、疲倦

和过错胡撒乱泼；

我渴望那斑斑

泪痕，那几乎爱得

太过分的印记，

那苦树皮和燃烧的

丁香发出的香气。

When stiff and sore and scarred

I take away my hand

From leaning on it hard

In grass and sand,

The hurt is not enough:

I long for weight and strength

To feel the earth as rough

To all my length.

我的手僵硬酸痛，布满伤痕，

于是我把它抽回，

不再依靠它使劲

撑进草丛和沙堆，

伤痛还不足够：

我渴望着重量和力道，

好以我的全部长度

去感受土地的粗糙。

The Kitchen Chimney

Builder, in building the little house,

In every way you may please yourself;

But please please me in the kitchen chimney:

Don't build me a chimney upon a shelf.

However far you must go for bricks,

Whatever they cost apiece or a pound,

Buy me enough for a full-length chimney,

And build the chimney clear from the ground.

It's not that I'm greatly afraid of fire,

But I never heard of a house that throve

(And I know of one that didn't thrive)

Where the chimney started above the stove.

厨房烟囱

建筑工,盖这座小房子,

随便你怎样让自己高兴;

但厨房烟囱一定要如我所愿:

不要在搁板上给我砌烟囱。

无论你要跑多远去找砖块,

无论要花一个硬币还是一镑,

给我买够砖,砌一根整长的烟囱,

把烟囱直接建在地面上。

倒不是说我特别怕火,

而是我从未听说哪座兴旺宅子

(我知道有一家就不怎么旺)

烟囱会从炉台以上开始。

And I dread the ominous stain of tar

That there always is on the papered walls,

And the smell of fire drowned in rain

That there always is when the chimney's false.

A shelf's for a clock or vase or picture,

But I don't see why it should have to bear

A chimney that only would serve to remind me

Of castles I used to build in air.

而且我害怕不吉利的焦油斑渍

总是沾上裱了纸的墙,

还有雨水浸灭炉火的味道,

烟囱建得不对时总是这样。

搁板本该摆放座钟、花瓶或照片,

但我想不通它为什么要

承担一根烟囱,那只会让我想起

我过去建在空中的城堡。

Looking for a Sunset Bird in Winter

The west was getting out of gold,

The breath of air had died of cold,

When shoeing home across the white,

I thought I saw a bird alight.

In summer when I passed the place,

I had to stop and lift my face;

A bird with an angelic gift

Was singing in it sweet and swift.

No bird was singing in it now.

A single leaf was on a bough,

And that was all there was to see

In going twice around the tree.

冬日黄昏寻鸟

西天的金色正在消散,

新鲜的空气已凝止于严寒,

穿过白雪走回家的时刻,

我想我看见了一只鸟飞落。

夏日里每次经过这个地方,

我都会停下来仰起脸庞;

一只天赋异禀的鸟

正在树上歌唱,轻快美妙。

现在树上没有鸟在唱。

一片孤叶挂在粗枝上,

绕树走了两圈,那就是

这里全部可看的东西。

From my advantage on a hill

I judged that such a crystal chill

Was only adding frost to snow

As gilt to gold that wouldn't show.

A brush had left a crooked stroke

Of what was either cloud or smoke

From north to south across the blue;

A piercing little star was through.

在山丘上凭高俯瞰，

我判断如此晶莹的严寒

不过是雪上再加霜，

仿佛金上镀金，并不显扬。

一支画笔留下弯弯的一划，

要么是云，要么是烟霞，

从北到南横过蔚蓝；

一颗锐利的小星贯穿。

Gathering Leaves

Spades take up leaves

No better than spoons,

And bags full of leaves

Are light as balloons.

I make a great noise

Of rustling all day

Like rabbit and deer

Running away.

But the mountains I raise

Elude my embrace,

Flowing over my arms

And into my face.

收集落叶

铁锨铲落叶

不如勺子好用,

装满落叶的袋子

像气球一样轻。

我整天发出

窸窸窣窣的噪音,

好像兔子和鹿

在逃遁。

但我捧起的小山

从我怀抱挣脱,

流过我的双臂

向我脸上掉落。

I may load and unload

Again and again

Till I fill the whole shed,

And what have I then?

Next to nothing for weight;

And since they grew duller

From contact with earth,

Next to nothing for color.

Next to nothing for use.

But a crop is a crop,

And who's to say where

The harvest shall stop?

我会一趟又一趟

装车又卸车，

直到填满整个棚子，

而我拥有了什么？

几乎没有重量；

因为和土地接触过

它们愈发暗淡，

几乎没有颜色。

几乎没有用处。

但收成就是收成，

谁又能说清楚

收获到哪儿该停？

On a Tree Fallen Across the Road

To hear us talk

The tree the tempest with a crash of wood

Throws down in front of us is not to bar

Our passage to our journey's end for good,

But just to ask us who we think we are

Insisting always on our own way so.

She likes to halt us in our runner tracks,

And make us get down in a foot of snow

Debating what to do without an ax.

And yet she knows obstruction is in vain:

We will not be put off the final goal

关于一棵横倒在路上的树
听我们说话

这棵暴风雪咔嚓一声折断

抛到我们面前的树,并非

永远阻挡我们去往旅程终点,

而只是问我们,我们以为自己是谁,

对自己的路总是这般坚持。

她喜欢把我们阻止在车辙间,

让我们下来,踏进一英尺深的雪里

争论没有斧头我们该怎么办。

然而她知道阻拦也是徒劳:

我们不会从最终的目标偏离,

We have it hidden in us to attain,

Not though we have to seize earth by the pole

And, tired of aimless circling in one place,

Steer straight off after something into space.

我们把它深藏在内心去达到,

哪怕为了抓住地球必须去地极,

而且,厌倦了漫无目的地原地转悠,

径直驶入太空去将某种东西追求。

The Need of Being Versed in Country Things

The house had gone to bring again

To the midnight sky a sunset glow.

Now the chimney was all of the house that stood,

Like a pistil after the petals go.

The barn opposed across the way,

That would have joined the house in flame

Had it been the will of the wind, was left

To bear forsaken the place's name.

No more it opened with all one end

For teams that came by the stony road

To drum on the floor with scurrying hoofs

And brush the mow with the summer load.

Robert Frost
A Witness Tree

精通乡下事务之必要

房子已烧掉,为午夜的天空

再一次带来落日的金晖。

如今只剩下烟囱兀立着,

仿佛花瓣落尽后的花蕊。

假如不是风的意愿,

路对面的谷仓早就和房子一同

毁于大火,现在它留下来

独自顶着废弃的地名。

它再不会将一侧完全敞开

迎接石路上过来的一队队大车,

马蹄匆匆敲击着地面,

满载夏日的收获掠过干草垛。

The birds that came to it through the air

At broken windows flew out and in,

Their murmur more like the sigh we sigh

From too much dwelling on what has been.

Yet for them the lilac renewed its leaf,

And the aged elm, though touched with fire;

And the dry pump flung up an awkward arm;

And the fence post carried a strand of wire.

For them there was really nothing sad.

But though they rejoiced in the nest they kept,

One had to be versed in country things

Not to believe the phoebes wept.

鸟儿穿过天空来到这里，

从残破的窗子飞进又飞出，

它们的咕哝更像是我们的叹息

因为耽溺于过往而倾吐。

然而丁香为它们发出新叶，

老榆树也一样，虽然曾被火舌触及；

枯涸的压水井尴尬地扬起臂膊；

篱笆桩上还缠着一段铁丝。

它们真的没什么可悲伤的。

尽管幸存的鸟巢让它们欢喜，

人还是得精通些乡下事务

才不至于相信菲比鹟会哭泣。

A Minor Bird

I have wished a bird would fly away,

And not sing by my house all day;

Have clapped my hands at him from the door

When it seemed as if I could bear no more.

The fault must partly have been in me.

The bird was not to blame for his key.

And of course there must be something wrong

In wanting to silence any song.

一只小鸟

我曾经盼望一只鸟儿飞走,

不要整天在我房前唱个不休;

当我似乎再也不能忍受,

我曾经从门口朝他拍手。

责任肯定有一部分在我。

鸟儿不该为唱出的曲调受谴责。

当然,想让任何歌唱噤声,

肯定是哪儿出了毛病。

Tree at My Window

Tree at my window, window tree,

My sash is lowered when night comes on;

But let there never be curtain drawn

Between you and me.

Vague dream-head lifted out of the ground,

And thing next most diffuse to cloud,

Not all your light tongues talking aloud

Could be profound.

But, tree, I have seen you taken and tossed,

And if you have seen me when I slept,

You have seen me when I was taken and swept

And all but lost.

我窗前的树

我窗前的树,窗前树,

夜晚来临时我拉下窗扇;

但是永远不要在你我之间

拉上帘幕。

迷蒙如梦的头① 拔地而起,

最近处的东西弥散到云端,

你片片轻薄舌头的阔论高谈

不可能全都精辟。

但是,树,我见过你被控制、颠簸,

你若是见过我睡觉的模样,

你就见过我被控制、涤荡,

几乎迷失自我。

---

① 指树冠。

That day she put our heads together,

Fate had her imagination about her,

Your head so much concerned with outer,

Mine with inner, weather.

那天命运把我们的头放在一处，

她有着关于自己的想象，

你的头如此关心外部的气象，

我的关注则在内部。

A Winter Eden

A winter garden in an alder swamp,

Where conies now come out to sun and romp,

As near a paradise as it can be

And not melt snow or start a dormant tree.

It lifts existence on a plane of snow

One level higher than the earth below,

One level nearer heaven overhead,

And last year's berries shining scarlet red.

It lifts a gaunt luxuriating beast

Where he can stretch and hold his highest feast

On some wild apple-tree's young tender bark,

What well may prove the year's high girdle mark.

冬日伊甸园

桤木沼泽中一座冬日的园子,
兔子们出来在阳光下嬉戏,
它现在最接近一座乐园,
雪尚未消融,树还在休眠。

它将生存提升到积雪层,
比下面的土地高了一层,
离头顶的天空近了一层,
去年的莓子闪耀着猩红。

它托起一头会享受的瘦弱野兽,
让他在野苹果树鲜嫩的树皮上头
可以够得到最高处的美食,
那将成为本年度最高环状标记。

So near to paradise all pairing ends:

Here loveless birds now flock as winter friends,

Content with bud-inspecting. They presume

To say which buds are leaf and which are bloom.

A feather-hammer gives a double knock.

This Eden day is done at two o'clock.

An hour of winter day might seem too short

To make it worth life's while to wake and sport.

如此接近乐园,所有欢会终止:

无爱的鸟儿作为冬日的朋友来此群集,

满足于检查幼芽。他们妄加

推测,哪些芽是叶子,哪些会开花。

一把羽毛锤子① 连敲两声。

这伊甸园的一天终结于两点钟。

冬天的白昼时光可能看上去太短,

不值得花去一段生命,醒来嬉玩。

---

① 指啄木鸟。

gaunt

ng

e

ch

his

east

wild

e's

nder

ll

e the

gh

ark.

Acquainted with the Night

I have been one acquainted with the night.

I have walked out in rain — and back in rain.

I have outwalked the furthest city light.

I have looked down the saddest city lane.

I have passed by the watchman on his beat

And dropped my eyes, unwilling to explain.

I have stood still and stopped the sound of feet

When far away an interrupted cry

Came over houses from another street,

熟悉黑夜

我曾是熟悉黑夜的一个。

我曾冒雨走出 —— 又冒雨返回。

我曾走出城市最远的灯火。

我曾望进城市最悲哀的巷子。

我曾路过当班巡逻的守夜人

并垂下眼睛,不愿解释。

我曾站立不动,止住脚步声,

此时远处一阵断续的哭喊

从另一条街传来,越过屋宇重重,

But not to call me back or say good-by;

And further still at an unearthly height

One luminary clock against the sky

Proclaimed the time was neither wrong nor right.

I have been one acquainted with the night.

但不是唤我回去或是道再见；

而更远处，在不可企及的高度，

一只发光的时钟挂在天边，

宣告时间既不错误也不正确。

我曾是熟悉黑夜的一个。

The Last Mowing

There's a place called Faraway Meadow

We never shall mow in again,

Or such is the talk at the farmhouse:

The meadow is finished with men.

Then now is the chance for the flowers

That can't stand mowers and plowers.

It must be now, though, in season

Before the not mowing brings trees on,

Before trees, seeing the opening,

March into a shadowy claim.

The trees are all I'm afraid of,

That flowers can't bloom in the shade of;

It's no more men I'm afraid of;

The meadow is done with the tame.

The place for the moment is ours

最后的割草

有一个地方叫作遥远牧场，

我们再不会去那里割草，

或者说农舍里是这么讲的：

牧场不再跟人打交道。

那么现在花儿有了机会，

割草机和耕犁让它们受够了罪。

不过必须趁现在，趁着正当季，

趁着不再割草还没有让树长起，

趁着树还没有看见开阔地，

长驱直入遮上浓荫。

我担心的就是这些树，

花儿在树荫下无法盛开；

我担心的已经不再是人；

牧场被驯服的日子已经结束。

此刻这地方属于我们，

For you, O tumultuous flowers,

To go to waste and go wild in,

All shapes and colors of flowers,

I needn't call you by name.

只为了你们，哦，喧闹的花儿，

去糟蹋，去恣意妄为，

各种形状和颜色的花儿，

我不必将你们的名字说出。

The Birthplace

Here further up the mountain slope

Than there was never any hope,

My father built, enclosed a spring,

Strung chains of wall round everything,

Subdued the growth of earth to grass,

And brought our various lives to pass.

A dozen girls and boys we were.

The mountain seemed to like the stir,

And made of us a little while—

With always something in her smile.

Today she wouldn't know our name.

(No girl's, of course, has stayed the same.)

The mountain pushed us off her knees.

And now her lap is full of trees.

出生地

在这远处于山坡之上

没有任何希望的地方,

绕着一眼清泉,我父亲筑起

一串围墙,圈住了所有东西,

抑制土地上的荒草生长,

将我们各式各样的生命带到世上。

我们有十几个姊妹弟兄。

大山似乎很喜欢这种骚动,

没多久就和我们相识——

她的微笑里总含有某种东西。

如今她叫不出我们的名字。

(当然,女孩们都已不用原来的姓氏。①)

大山将我们从膝上推走。

现在树长满了她膝头。

---

① 意思是,女孩们都已结婚,改随夫姓。

Sitting by a Bush in Broad Sunlight

When I spread out my hand here today,

I catch no more than a ray

To feel of between thumb and fingers;

No lasting effect of it lingers.

There was one time and only the one

When dust really took in the sun;

And from that one intake of fire

All creatures still warmly suspire.

And if men have watched a long time

And never seen sun-smitten slime

Again come to life and crawl off,

We must not be too ready to scoff.

晴日灌木林边小坐

今天我在这里摊开手掌，

只不过抓住一束阳光

在拇指和四指之间感受；

没有什么持久的效果存留。

曾经有一次，唯一的一次，

尘土真的将阳光吸取；

就凭着那一次火的摄取

一切生灵仍在温暖地呼吸。①

假如人们经过长时间观察

也没见泥浆经阳光抽打

而重获生命，然后爬开掉，

我们也不必急于嘲笑。

① 此处指上帝用尘土造人。见《旧约·创世记》。

God once declared He was true

And then took the veil and withdrew,

And remember how final a hush

Then descended of old on the bush.

God once spoke to people by name.

The sun once imparted its flame.

One impulse persists as our breath;

The other persists as our faith.

上帝曾宣称他是真实存在

然后遮上帐幕隐身离开，

要记住何等终极的宁静

随之降临在昔日的荆棘丛。①

上帝曾指名与人交谈。

太阳曾给予它的光焰。

一种冲动延续成我们的生命；

我们的信仰源于另一种冲动。

---

① 此处指上帝在荆棘丛中向摩西显形。见《旧约·出埃及记》。

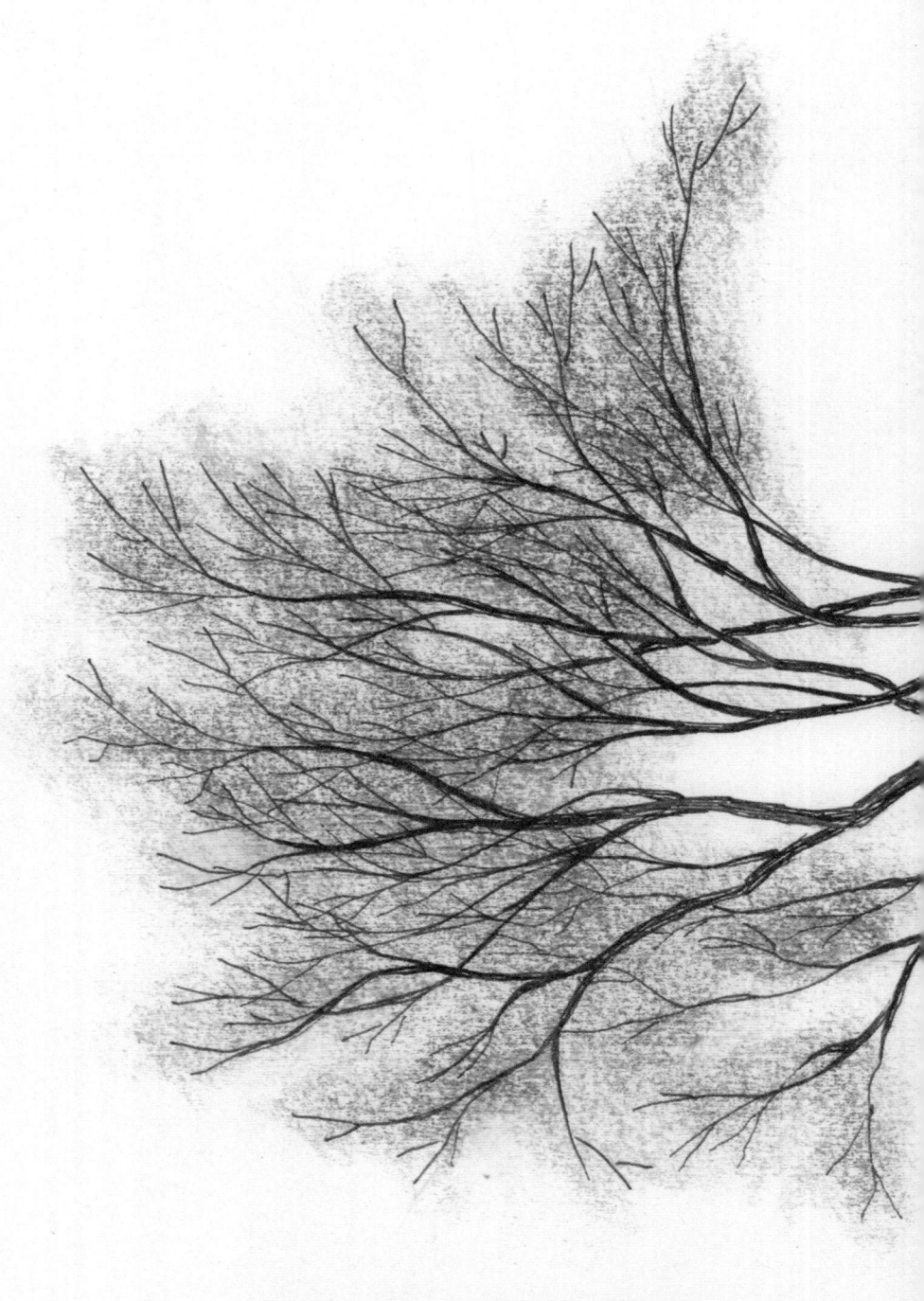

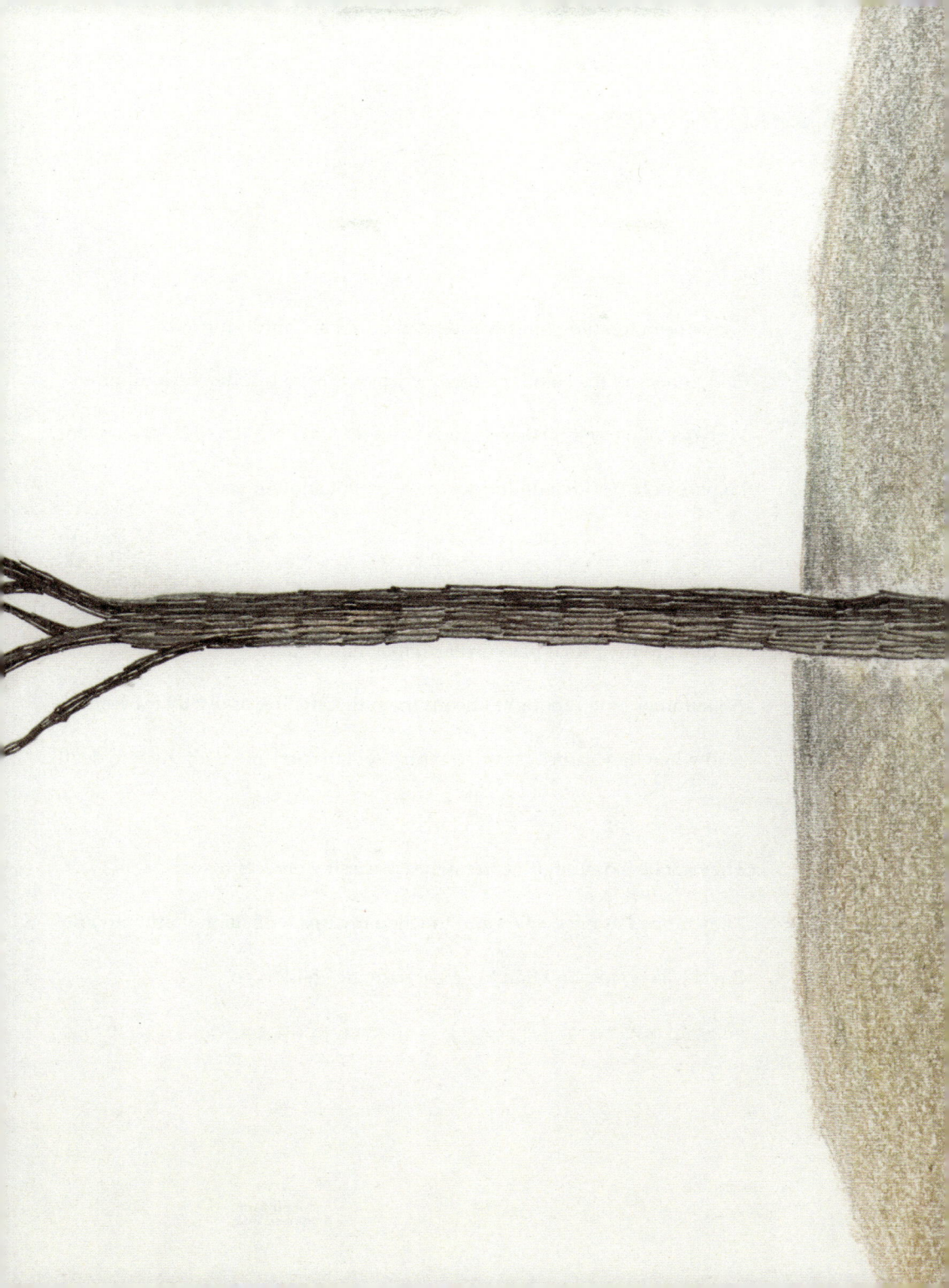

A Leaf-Treader

I have been treading on leaves all day until I am autumn-tired.

God knows all the color and form of leaves I have trodden on and mired.

Perhaps I have put forth too much strength and been too fierce from fear.

I have safely trodden underfoot the leaves of another year.

All summer long they were over head, more lifted up than I.

To come to their final place in earth they had to pass me by.

All summer long I thought I heard them threatening under their breath.

And when they came it seemed with a will to carry me with them to death.

They spoke to the fugitive in my heart as if it were leaf to leaf.

They tapped at my eyelids and touched my lips with an invitation to grief.

But it was no reason I had to go because they had to go.

Now up my knee to keep on top of another year of snow.

踏叶人

我整天踩踏落叶,直到我厌烦了秋季。

上帝知道有多少颜色和形状的落叶被我踩踏成泥。

也许我太过用力,这般残忍是出于恐惧。

我已将又一年的落叶稳稳地踩在脚底。

整个夏天它们在头顶高悬,高出我许多。

为了前往泥土里的归宿,它们从我身旁经过。

整个夏天我都觉得听见了它们的低声威胁。

它们经过时,似乎有意拖着我一同死灭。

它们对我内心的逃犯讲话,就好像树叶对树叶。

它们敲打我眼睑、碰触我嘴唇,发出悲伤的邀约。

但没有这样的道理,因为它们要走,我就得坠落。

现在抬起来吧,我的膝盖,去凌驾又一年的雪。

Neither Out Far Nor In Deep

The people along the sand

All turn and look one way.

They turn their back on the land.

They look at the sea all day.

As long as it takes to pass

A ship keeps raising its hull;

The wetter ground like glass

Reflects a standing gull.

The land may vary more;

But wherever the truth may be—

The water comes ashore,

And the people look at the sea.

不远也不深

人们沿沙滩而立,

都转头看着一个方向。

他们背弃了陆地。

他们整天望着海洋。

只要远处驶来一艘船

它的船身就不断升起;

地面更湿了,好像玻璃板

映出一只海鸥独立。

陆地可能更为多变;

但不管真理可能在何方——

海水总是涌向海岸,

人们总是望着海洋。

They cannot look out far.

They cannot look in deep.

But when was that ever a bar

To any watch they keep?

向外他们看不远。

向内他们看不深。

但何尝有障碍遮拦

他们坚持观望的眼神?

Beech

Where my imaginary line

Bends square in woods, an iron spine

And pile of real rocks have been founded.

And off this corner in the wild,

Where these are driven in and piled,

One tree, by being deeply wounded,

Has been impressed as Witness Tree

And made commit to memory

My proof of being not unbounded.

Thus truth's established and borne out,

Though circumstanced with dark and doubt—

Though by a world of doubt surrounded.

—*The Moodie Forester*

山毛榉

我的假想线在树林里

折成方形的地方,一根铁脊

和一堆真正的石块已经竖起。

在这荒野的一角以外,

这些东西被运进、堆放的地方,

一棵树,曾经被割出深深的伤口,

由此标记为"见证树"①,

让我并非没有边界的证据

得以提交给记忆。

就这样真相确立并得到证明,

尽管处于黑暗和怀疑的环境之中——

尽管为一个怀疑的世界所包围。

——穆迪·弗雷斯特②

① 人们在勘察土地时,习惯于将一棵树剥去部分树皮、刻上标记,作为界桩,称作"见证树",又称"标志树"。
② "穆迪"是弗罗斯特母亲婚前的姓氏;"弗雷斯特"意为"护林人"。

Come In

As I came to the edge of the woods,

Thrush music — hark!

Now if it was dusk outside,

Inside it was dark.

Too dark in the woods for a bird

By sleight of wing

To better its perch for the night,

Though it still could sing.

The last of the light of the sun

That had died in the west

Still lived for one song more

In a thrush's breast.

请进

当我来到树林的边缘,

听 —— 画眉鸣啭!

此刻假如外面是黄昏,

树林里就是黑暗。

树林对于鸟儿太过黑暗,

凭借翅膀的敏捷

它找不到更好的栖枝过夜,

尽管它还能唱歌。

太阳消逝在西天的

最后一道光芒

还残留着再听一支歌

在那画眉的胸膛。

Far in the pillared dark

Thrush music went—

Almost like a call to come in

To the dark and lament.

But no, I was out for stars:

I would not come in.

I meant not even if asked,

And I hadn't been.

远在廊柱撑起的黑暗中

画眉在鸣啭——

几乎像一声召唤，邀请

进入黑暗哀叹。

但是不，我出来是为看星星：

我是不会进去的。

我是说即便受到邀请也不去，

况且没有谁请我。

A Young Birch

The birch begins to crack its outer sheath

Of baby green and show the white beneath,

As whosoever likes the young and slight

May well have noticed. Soon entirely white

To double day and cut in half the dark

It will stand forth, entirely white in bark,

And nothing but the top leafy green —

The only native tree that dares to lean,

Relying on its beauty, to the air.

(Less brave perhaps than trusting are the fair.)

And someone reminiscent will recall

How once in cutting brush along the wall

He spared it from the number of the slain,

At first to be no bigger than a cane,

And then no bigger than a fishing pole,

一棵小白桦

白桦开始裂开它嫩绿色的

外鞘,露出底下的白色,

任谁对幼小和纤弱者喜爱

都会注意到。不久就会全变白,

让白日加倍,将黑暗减半,

它会挺起,树皮纯白一片,

浑身只有树冠是叶绿——

本地树里唯一的一棵,敢于

凭借它的美,倾向于天空

(也许公平讲,与其说勇敢毋宁是信任。)

某个沉湎往事的人会记起

有一次沿着墙根砍掉灌木时

他把它从那些受害者中抽出,

一开始都不比一根藤条粗

后来也不能胜过一根钓鱼竿,

But now at last so obvious a bole

The most efficient help you ever hired

Would know that it was there to be admired,

And zeal would not be thanked that cut it down

When you were reading books or out of town.

It was a thing of beauty and was sent

To live its life out as an ornament.

现在终于明显长成了树干，

你能雇到的最高效的帮工

都知道它在那儿就是要受爱敬，

要是趁着你读书或者出城

砍倒它，这份热忱可没人领情。

它是一件美的事物，注定

要作为一件装饰品度过一生。

Away !

Now I out walking

The world desert,

And my shoe and my stocking

Do me no hurt.

I leave behind

Good friends in town.

Let them get well-wined

And go lie down.

Don't think I leave

For the outer dark

Like Adam and Eve

Put out of the Park.

离去!

现在我出去

走这世界的荒漠,

有了我的鞋子和袜子

它伤不到我。

我把好朋友

留在身后的城里。

随他们痛饮美酒

再躺倒休息。

不要以为我离家

是为了外面的黑暗,

就像亚当和夏娃

被逐出乐园。

Forget the myth.

There is no one I

Am put out with

Or put out by.

Unless I'm wrong

I but obey

The urge of a song:

"I'm — bound — away!"

And I may return

If dissatisfied

With what I learn

From having died.

那神话无须理会。

并没有哪一个

与我相伴相随

或者驱逐我。

除非我理解错误，

否则我唯有谨依

一首歌的敦促：

"我——将——离——去！"

我也许还会回转，

假如我不满意

从自己的死亡里面

学到的东西。

Forgive, O Lord...

Forgive, O Lord, my little jokes on Thee

And I'll forgive Thy great big one on me.

哦主，请原谅……

哦主，请原谅我对你开的小玩笑，
我也原谅你对我开的大玩笑。

In Winter in the Woods...

In winter in the woods alone

Against the trees I go.

I mark a maple for my own

And lay the maple low.

At four o'clock I shoulder ax,

And in the afterglow

I link a line of shadowy tracks

Across the tinted snow.

I see for Nature no defeat

In one tree's overthrow

Or for myself in my retreat

For yet another blow.

冬日独自在林里……

冬日独自在林里

我准备对树不利。

我标好一棵枫树给自己

然后将它砍倒在地。

四点钟,我扛起斧子,

在落日余晖里

我穿过染了色的雪地

串起一行带影子的足迹。

我不会将一棵树的倒地

看作自然的失利,

我的退却也并非失利,

而是为了再一次打击。

图书在版编目（CIP）数据

见证树：弗罗斯特诗选 /（美）罗伯特·弗罗斯特著；雷格译；闻燕绘 . — 北京：国际文化出版公司，2021.10
 ISBN 978-7-5125-1325-9

 I. ①见⋯ II. ①罗⋯ ②雷⋯ ③闻⋯ III. ①抒情诗－作品集－美国－近代 IV. ① I712.24

中国版本图书馆 CIP 数据核字（2021）第 162362 号

见证树：弗罗斯特诗选

作　　者	[美]罗伯特·弗罗斯特
译　　者	雷　格
绘　　者	闻　燕
责任编辑	侯娟雅
特约编辑	文　雯　窦雅倩
统筹监制	文　钊
策划编辑	邓锦辉　文　雯
装帧设计	今亮後聲 HOPESOUND 2580590616@qq.com ·张今亮　核漫
出版发行	国际文化出版公司
经　　销	全国新华书店
印　　刷	天津市祥丰印务有限公司
开　　本	710 毫米 ×1000 毫米　16 开 13.5 印张　　　　152 千字
版　　次	2021 年 10 月第 1 版 2021 年 10 月第 1 次印刷
书　　号	ISBN 978-7-5125-1325-9
定　　价	68.00 元

国际文化出版公司
北京朝阳区东土城路乙 9 号　　邮编：100013
总编室：（010）64271187　　传真：（010）64271578
销售热线：（010）64271187
传真：（010）64271187－800
E-mail：icpc@95777.sina.net